CUBANS IN AMERICA

web enhanced at www.inamericabooks.com

LEE ENGFER

LERNER PUBLICATIONS COMPANY / MINNEAPOLIS

Current information and statistics quickly become out of date. That's why we developed **www.inamericabooks.com**, a companion website to the **In America** series. The site offers lots of additional information—downloadable photos and maps and up-to-date facts through links to additional websites. Each link has been carefully selected by researchers at Lerner Publishing Group and is regularly reviewed and updated. However, Lerner Publishing Group is not responsible for the accuracy or suitability of material on websites that are not maintained directly by us. It is recommended that students using the Internet be supervised by a parent, a librarian, a teacher, or another adult.

Lerner Publications Company
A division of Lerner Publishing Group
241 First Avenue North
Minneapolis, MN 55401 U.S.A.

Website address: www.lernerbooks.com

Library of Congress Cataloging-in-Publication Data
Engfer, Lee, 1963-
Cubans in America / by Lee Engfer.
p. cm. — (In America)
Includes bibliographical references and index.
ISBN: 0-8225-4870-4 (lib. bdg. : alk. paper)
1. Cuban Americans–History–Juvenile literature. 2. Immigrants–United States–History–Juvenile literature. 3. Cuban Americans–Juvenile literature. I. Title. II. Series: In America (Minneapolis, Minn.)
E184.C97E54 2005
973'.04687291–dc22 2004025095

Manufactured in the United States of America
1 2 3 4 5 6 – JR – 10 09 08 07 06 05

Contents

INTRODUCTION

In America, a walk down a city street can seem like a walk through many lands. Grocery stores sell international foods. Shops offer products from around the world. People strolling past may speak foreign languages. This unique blend of cultures is the result of America's history as a nation of immigrants.

Native peoples have lived in North America for centuries. The next settlers were the Vikings. In about A.D. 1000, they sailed from Scandinavia to lands that would become Canada, Greenland, and Iceland. In 1492 the Italian navigator Christopher Columbus landed in the Americas, and more European explorers arrived during the 1500s. In the 1600s, British settlers formed colonies that, after the Revolutionary War (1775–1783), would become the United States. And in the mid-1800s, a great wave of immigration brought millions of new arrivals to the young country.

Immigrants have many different reasons for leaving home. They may leave to escape poverty, war, or harsh governments. They may want better living conditions for themselves and their children. Throughout its history, America has been known as a nation that offers many opportunities. For this reason, many immigrants come to America.

Moving to a new country is not easy. It can mean making a long, difficult journey. It means leaving home and starting over in an unfamiliar place. But it also means using skill, talent, and determination to build a new life. The In America series tells the story of immigration to the United States and the search for fresh beginnings in a new country—in America.

Cubans in America

Cuba is a narrow, alligator-shaped island in the Caribbean Sea between the U.S. coast of Florida and the Yucatán Peninsula of Mexico. Just ninety miles separate Cuba from the United States. The two countries have been closely linked ever since the 1500s, when Spain established colonies in Cuba and Florida. The U.S. economy often controlled Cuba's fortunes, and neither nation has been able to ignore the other.

The two countries clashed after Cuban revolutionary leader Fidel Castro seized power in 1959. Castro embraced Communism, a political and economic system in which the government controls resources. The United States viewed Communism as a threat to democracy. Growing tensions led to U.S. limits on trade with and travel to Cuba.

While Cubans have been coming to America since the days of Spanish rule, by far the largest number arrived after Castro took power. In the decades following Castro's revolution, more than one million people left the island. This "great migration" is known in Spanish as *el exilio*, or "exile." Cubans were exiled—forced to leave their homeland—because of bitter disagreement with Castro's government. This sense of exile colors the Cuban experience in America.

In 1959, the year of the revolution in Cuba, an estimated 124,000 Cubans were living in the United States. By the early twenty-first century. the Cuban American population had grown ten times as large, to about 1.2 million. Cuban Americans make up less than 1 percent of the U.S. population, but they are among the most successful and politically active of recent immigrants. They have excelled in politics, music, sports, business, and other fields. They continue to stand up for freedom and dream of a more democratic Cuba, even as America has become home.

1 The Beautiful Island

The largest of four islands that make up the Greater Antilles chain, Cuba is known as the Pearl of the Antilles because of its lush green scenery. Much of the island consists of fields and gently rolling hills. Cuba's pleasant climate features warm temperatures year-round, with dry and rainy seasons. Havana is the nation's capital and largest city.

The First Cubans

As early as 3500 B.C., various groups of people had moved to the Antilles and other Caribbean islands from South, Central, and North America. These early peoples traveled in canoes from island to island.

In Cuba the Ciboney people settled near the coast and rivers, where they fished and used shells

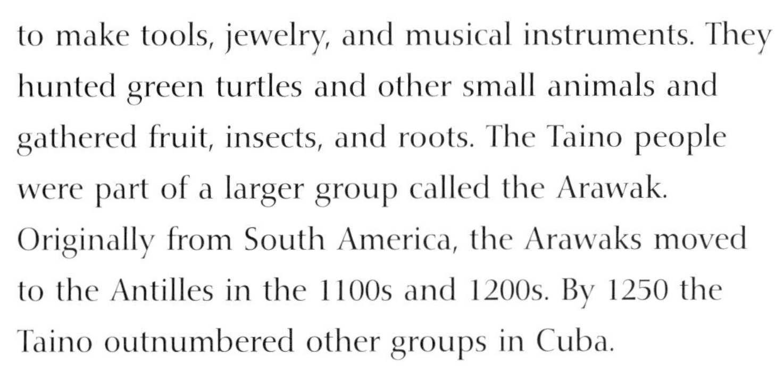

to make tools, jewelry, and musical instruments. They hunted green turtles and other small animals and gathered fruit, insects, and roots. The Taino people were part of a larger group called the Arawak. Originally from South America, the Arawaks moved to the Antilles in the 1100s and 1200s. By 1250 the Taino outnumbered other groups in Cuba.

The Taino lived mostly in the highlands of eastern Cuba. They settled in towns built around a main square, in houses made from palm leaves. The people carved stone tools and grew a variety of crops, including yucca (a starchy root vegetable), tobacco, boniato (a kind of sweet potato), and corn.

Christopher Columbus landed on the eastern shores of Cuba on October 28, 1492. He described the island as "the most beautiful land that human eyes have ever seen." At the time, about 100,000 native people (called Indians by the Europeans) were living on the palm-covered island.

A statue of Christopher Columbus in Baracoa, Cuba, marks the explorer's landing in eastern Cuba, in 1492. Baracoa was one of the first Spanish settlements in Cuba.

Spanish Colony

Columbus returned to Cuba in 1494 and explored the western side of the island. He claimed the island for the king and queen of Spain, who were financing Columbus's expeditions to the "New World," or Western Hemisphere. At the time, the Caribbean island of Hispaniola

served as Spain's base of operations in the Americas.

In the early 1500s, the Spanish governor of Hispaniola sent Diego Velázquez to Cuba to lead the conquest of the island. By 1514 Velázquez had defeated the native people and established settlements at Baracoa, Bayamo, Havana, Puerto Príncipe, Trinidad, Sancti Spíritus, and Santiago de Cuba. During the colonial period, a series of captain generals, leaders appointed by the Spanish government, held power in Cuba. Roman Catholic missionaries and priests were among the first colonists, as the Spanish brought their religion to the New World and worked to convert the native people to Catholicism.

In Cuba, as in other Spanish colonies in the Caribbean, two main forces drove the economy: sugar and slavery. Soon after taking over Cuba, the Spanish began growing sugarcane and milling sugar. At first, the Spanish forced the Taino to harvest the sugarcane. But the native population of Cuba was soon destroyed. Hard labor killed many of the people, and thousands died from diseases brought to the island by the Europeans.

To meet the demand for workers, landowners began importing slaves from Africa. Most of the farmers in Cuba were criollos, people of Spanish descent who were born in Cuba. In 1792 a slave revolt in the nearby nation of Haiti nearly ruined Haiti's sugar industry. Cuban sugarcane growers took advantage of the unrest in Haiti to expand their markets.

By 1806 Cuba had replaced Haiti as the major sugar manufacturer in the Caribbean and the third largest sugar producer in the world. Cuban sugarcane growers established plantations, large agricultural estates operated by slave labor. Cuban plantation owners imported close to one million slaves from Africa to the island during the 1800s. The sugarcane growers also brought in workers from China, adding a new element to Cuba's diverse population.

African slaves were not permitted to practice their own religions in

Harvesting sugarcane wasn't the only job slaves had to do in Cuba. The Spanish colonists also used slaves to mine for gold, as shown in the drawing above.

Spanish-controlled Cuba. But they held on to their beliefs by disguising their deities—spirit gods called orishas—in the identities of Roman Catholic saints. This fusion of Catholicism and African religious beliefs became known as Santeria.

The slave trade created a society in which black and mixed-race people outnumbered the white criollos and the *peninsulares,* Spanish-born citizens living in Cuba. The criollos feared that Cuba would follow the path of Haiti, where the slave revolt had led to the loss of prestige and property for criollos. For their own protection, the Cuban criollos chose to maintain close ties to Spain, even though they felt they were treated unjustly by the Spanish governors.

Some criollos, however, began to question the harsh treatment of slaves. Workers on sugar plantations labored from dawn to dusk and lived in cramped quarters. Other criollos objected to Spanish control of many aspects of life on the island. Cuban-born people were not allowed to hold government posts.

In 1823 an outspoken Cuban reformer and Catholic priest named Félix Varela fled to New York City to escape a death sentence imposed by the Spanish parliament. Over the years, other Cubans who favored

independence from Spain also came to New York. Some of them argued that Cuba should be annexed (joined) to the United States. Various attempts to encourage the U.S. purchase of Cuba fizzled, however.

THE EXILE KNOWS HIS PLACE, AND THAT PLACE IS THE IMAGINATION.

—Ricardo Pau-Llosa, Cuban American poet

The Struggle for Independence

As the nineteenth century wore on, tensions between Spaniards and Cubans increased. In 1868 a criollo plantation owner, Carlos Manuel de Céspedes, freed his own slaves and demanded freedom for all of Cuba's slaves. He also called for Cuba's independence from Spain. His battle cry, known as the Grito de Yara ("Cry of Yara," named for the town where Céspedes proclaimed independence), launched a rebel uprising in the eastern half of the colony. The conflict, known as the Ten Years' War (1868–1878), ended in 1878 with the rebels' defeat. The push for independence continued, however, along with the fight to end slavery, which was finally abolished in Cuba in 1886.

TO LEARN MORE ABOUT CUBA'S HISTORY, INCLUDING INFORMATION ABOUT THE SPANISH COLONIZATION OF THE ISLAND AND CUBA'S INDEPENDENCE MOVEMENT, CHECK OUT WWW.INAMERICABOOKS.COM FOR LINKS.

The Cuban independence movement operated not only in Cuba but also in New York City. In the face of increasing political, economic, and social turmoil in Cuba, more Cubans settled in the United States. Cuban cigar manufacturers opened factories in Key West and Tampa, Florida, to avoid paying high import taxes to sell cigars—one of Cuba's most celebrated products—in the United States. By the mid-1870s, forty-five cigar factories were operating in Key West. By 1880 the Cuban population in the United States was seven thousand, up from one thousand in the 1850s.

Cigar City

The Cuban cigar industry arrived in Florida in 1831, when fifty tobacco workers from Havana opened a cigar factory *(right)* in Key West. In the late 1860s, Vicente Martínez Ybor, a Spaniard who'd been brought up in Cuba, joined the ranks of the Key West cigar manufacturers. His factory was a success, but the lack of a freshwater supply led Ybor to look for a new location for his business.

In 1885 the cigar maker found his spot—a forty-acre swamp near Tampa. Tampa had a good harbor and a railroad for shipping, a freshwater well, and a warm, humid climate that was ideal for cigar making. Offering affordable housing and long-term employment, Ybor drew five thousand cigar factory workers to the area, which was known as Ybor City. By 1900 it was the Cigar Capital of the World, and Cubans made up more than 20 percent of Tampa's population.

Workers rolled cigars by hand and made attractive wooden cigar boxes. In the factories, *lectors* (readers) sat on a platform above the workers and read newspapers and literature out loud.

Ybor City, along with Key West, served as a major staging point for Cuban independence. Cigar factory lectors often read from revolutionary newspapers, and independence leader José Martí visited Ybor City several times. In 1893 Martí delivered a rousing speech to more than ten thousand Cubans gathered outside Ybor's cigar factory.

The most influential Cuban in America in the late 1800s was poet and author José Martí, who became known as the Father of Cuban Independence. Martí moved to New York City from Spain in 1880 after being exiled from Cuba for his anticolonial activities. Supported by other Cuban exiles in New York and Mexico, Martí organized a war for Cuban independence. In April 1895, he led an invasion force to the island to join Cuban troops who were already fighting.

José Martí

Known as the Father of Cuban Independence or the George Washington of Cuba, José Martí *(below)* was born in Havana in 1853. From an early age, Martí crusaded for Cuba's independence from Spain. When he was sixteen, he wrote a political essay that led to his conviction for treason, and in 1871 he was exiled to Spain. He returned to Cuba, only to be deported again. In 1880 Martí moved to New York City, where he wrote poetry, essays, and newspaper articles in support of a free Cuba.

In the United States, Martí united the Cuban exile community and organized a war for Cuba's independence. He traveled to Cuba in 1895 to lead the war, but he didn't live to see victory. He was killed in a skirmish just days after the war began. Martí's legacy as a freedom fighter lives on in both Cuba and Cuban American communities in the United States.

Martí was killed in battle just eight days later, but his death did not stop the rebels. After his death, Martí was revered as a martyr for Cuban independence.

As the war for independence waged on, Spanish forces slaughtered thousands of rebel troops. But the soldiers also targeted ordinary citizens, forcing hundreds of thousands of them into crowded prison camps that lacked proper sanitation and enough food. Many Cubans died of hunger and diseases.

Newspapers in the United States published many stories about these harsh measures. U.S. citizens were sympathetic to the Cubans' demands for independence and were horrified by stories of Spanish brutality. At the same time, Americans who owned land and businesses in Cuba, and those who did business with Cuba, feared that the explosive situation would affect them.

Responding to this pressure, U.S. president William McKinley sent the battleship *Maine* to Havana's harbor to protect U.S. citizens and property in Cuba. On February 15, 1898, the *Maine* blew up, and more than 250 crew members were killed. Although the cause of the explosion was never determined, the United States blamed Spanish forces.

On April 25, the United States declared war on Spain. The conflict, known in the United States as the Spanish-American War, was short, ending when Spain declared a cease-fire in August 1898. A treaty signed by Spain and the United States finally ended Spanish rule of Cuba. Spanish troops surrendered directly to

I AM FINALLY IN A COUNTRY WHERE EACH CAN BE HIS OWN MASTER. HERE ONE CAN BREATHE FREELY BECAUSE LIBERTY IS THE BASIS, THE SHIELD, THE VERY ESSENCE OF LIFE.

—José Martí, writing about his life in the United States

After the destruction of the U.S. battleship Maine (above), *tensions between Spain and the United States increased, though no evidence ever proved that Spanish forces caused the explosion.*

the United States, however, and no Cubans were present when the treaty was signed. After fighting so long and hard for their independence, Cubans were excluded from the process, and power shifted immediately to the United States.

From 1899 to 1902, a U.S. military government controlled Cuba, and the United States imported much of Cuba's sugar and tobacco. The U.S. government agreed to end its occupation of Cuba only after Cuban leaders agreed to a change in their new constitution. The Platt Amendment to the Cuban constitution allowed the United States to be involved in Cuba's political and military affairs. It also gave the United States the right to build a permanent naval base in Cuba. Finally, in early 1902,

FOR LINKS TO MORE INFORMATION ABOUT THE SPANISH-AMERICAN WAR, VISIT WWW.INAMERICABOOKS.COM.

Cuba became a self-governing republic, under the presidency of Tomás Estrada Palma, a Cuban who had lived in New York since the end of the Ten Years' War.

Daily Life in Cuba

In the early years of the twentieth century, the gap between rich and poor Cubans widened. Much of the land was owned by a few wealthy individuals or U.S. companies. The upper class gained power, while lower-class Cubans struggled to get by. For poor Cubans, life hadn't changed much since the days of Spanish rule. Large family groups—grandparents, aunts, uncles, cousins—lived together in cramped quarters, and many people were lucky just to have rice and beans to eat.

Many rural Cubans worked on farms and lived in *bohíos,* traditional thatch-roofed dwellings with dirt floors. Rural communities often lacked health care facilities, schools, decent roads, and housing. In cities, working-class people worked as taxi drivers, tour guides,

Many Cubans in rural areas still live in thatch-roofed dwellings that resemble the bohíos of their ancestors, the Taino.

and telephone and telegraph operators.

U.S. companies continued to buy land and businesses in Cuba, and trade and tourism flourished between the two countries. Many upper-class and middle-class Cubans learned English and began to embrace more aspects of American culture. By the early twentieth century, 50,000 to 100,000 people were traveling between the United States and Cuba each year. At the same time, Afro-Cubans (Cubans of African heritage) and other poor people began to resent Americans, as well as the Cuban upper class, seeing them as the enemy.

Despite the divisions in Cuban society, the people did share a common culture. Whatever their ethnic heritage—Spanish, African, Chinese, or mixed—all Cubans spoke Spanish. They placed a high value on family life, and extended families often lived together under one roof. Most Cubans followed the Roman Catholic religious faith, though many people practiced Santeria.

My grandfather, Manolo . . . and [his brother] José married two sisters, two Cuban-born daughters of Spaniards. Manolo had nine kids, José had six. And they lived in one house, with a common kitchen, a cook, and some maids, to take care of all of these kids. This family is still—I call them uncles and aunts, my second cousins. A very big, happy family.

—Rosa Vazquez

The blend of ethnicities in Cuba led to a vibrant cultural life, with a distinguished tradition in the arts, including painting, literature, and especially music. African slaves brought the rhythms, drums, and dances of Africa to Cuba, where they were blended with Spanish guitars and melodies. Cuban music featured guitars and percussion instruments

This couple shows off the rumba, a popular Cuban dance, in Miami Beach, Florida, in the 1930s.

such as castanets, maracas, and a variety of drums. Cuban music also gave rise to many different dances, such as the mambo, conga, rumba, and cha-cha.

Another aspect of Cuba's unique cultural mix was its cooking. Rice was the most common Cuban food, and many Cuban dishes were made with onions, green pepper, garlic, and tomatoes. Typical Cuban dishes included black beans and rice, fried plantains (bananas), chicken and rice, minced beef and rice, meat hash (called *ropa vieja*, meaning "old clothes"), boiled yucca, and yucca with garlic sauce. A special holiday meal was roast pork—a whole, roasted suckling pig—or a pot roast.

BÉISBOL

Baseball came to Cuba from the United States in the late 1800s and quickly became the favorite pastime on the island. The first Cubans to become celebrities in the United States were baseball players such as pitcher Ádolfo Luque, who played for twenty-one years beginning in 1914. By the end of the 1940s, forty-three Cubans had played in the major leagues.

When Cubans began playing béisbol in the United States, the game was segregated—only white players could be in the major leagues, while black players had a separate ball club, the Negro Leagues. In 1935 the Washington Senators signed a Cuban outfielder named Roberto Estralella. Like many Cubans, Estralella was of mixed Spanish and African ancestry. Although a person of African descent would have been forbidden to play in the majors, the Senators management got around the rule by saying that Estralella was Cuban, not black.

A REPUBLIC IN TURMOIL

After Cuba became an independent nation, its political situation remained unstable. A series of corrupt presidents ruled the country. In September 1933, an army sergeant named Fulgencio Batista seized control of the temporary government set up after the downfall of President Gerardo Machado. Batista dominated political life in Cuba until 1944, when Ramón Grau San Martín was elected president. Batista illegally seized power again in 1952.

Batista abused his power, appointing people to government posts in exchange for money. While the upper classes—landowners and businesspeople—grew rich under Batista, many Cubans continued to suffer from poverty, lack of health

This graffiti in Havana, Cuba, reads, "Down with Batista, assassin."

care, and inadequate schools. Even though Batista ruled as a dictator (a leader who holds complete, unlimited control), the U.S. government remained on friendly terms with him. U.S. businesses invested heavily in Cuban sugar production, agriculture, and utilities such as telephone companies.

Anyone who dared to oppose Batista was severely punished. His dictatorship was known for its inhuman prison cells, where hundreds of men and women died under torture. By the mid-1950s, Cuba was ripe for another revolution.

Castro's Revolution

On July 26, 1953, a young lawyer named Fidel Castro and a group of daring young men and women attacked the Moncada army barracks in Santiago de Cuba, a city in the eastern province of Oriente. Castro hoped to spark a popular uprising in Oriente that would lead to Batista's overthrow. Castro's plan was to seize arms from the barracks and enlist more volunteers for his revolutionary movement. His goal was a society in which everyone was equal. He called for more favorable working conditions for the Cuban people and reforms in education, housing, and land ownership.

Despite Castro's high expectations, the attack on the Moncada barracks failed. The odds were against

the rebels, since they numbered only about 130, while the barracks held more than 1,000 soldiers. Most of the rebels were jailed, tortured, or killed. Castro was captured, tried, and sentenced to fifteen years in prison. At his trial, Castro spoke brilliantly in his own defense. In the speech, entitled "History Will Absolve Me," he attacked the injustices of Batista's regime.

In 1955 Castro and other prisoners were pardoned and released. Shortly afterward, Castro left for Mexico to train soldiers for another attempt to oust Batista. His force would fight as guerrillas, independent soldiers waging attacks from a hideout in the mountains.

On board the ship *Granma,* Castro and eighty-one men landed on the coast of Oriente in early December 1956, full of high hopes of finally toppling Batista. But Batista's army had been warned of the invasion and overcame Castro in a surprise attack. The Rebel Army fled into nearby forests, and many rebels were shot or captured. Castro assembled the dozen or so survivors and established a hideaway in the Sierra Maestra, a forested mountain range.

Castro quickly gained the respect of people in the region, particularly the peasants, or campesinos, who helped him carry on his fight. Many other Cubans, including students, workers, and housewives, participated in the rebellion in the cities. They formed underground groups known as *el llano,* the urban guerrilla movement. During 1956 and 1957, these secret organizations placed bombs, organized strikes, and caused electricity blackouts (temporary power

outages) in major cities like Santiago and Havana.

Meanwhile, in the Sierra Maestra, Castro strengthened his position with the help of two key Rebel Army leaders, Ernesto "Che" Guevara and Camilo Cienfuegos. Guevara was an Argentinian doctor and revolutionary who had met Castro in Mexico and decided to join his cause. Cienfuegos, born in Camagüey, Cuba, was a popular leader. By late August 1958, Castro and his troops were ready to launch a final attack on Batista. Sensing his doom, on New Year's Eve 1958, Batista and his trusted advisers flew to the nearby Dominican Republic.

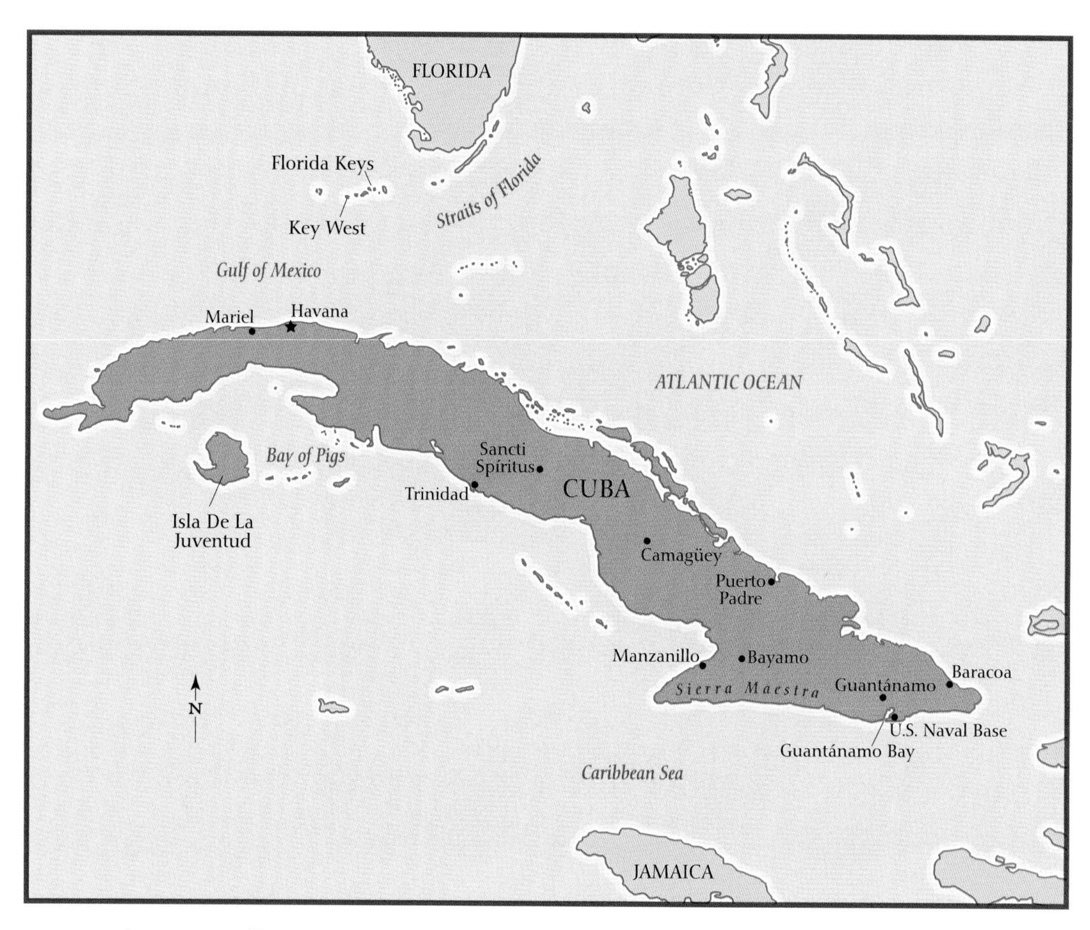

More than one million Cubans have left their homeland for the United States since 1959. Download this map of Cuba and other maps at www.inamericabooks.com.

Castro's revolutionaries seized power on January 1, 1959, at the dawn of the new year. On January 8, Castro made his triumphant entry into Havana along with the Rebel Army. Wearing beads around their necks and sporting long hair and beards, the rebels marched in the streets of Havana as residents jumped for joy and danced. Women hugged and kissed the bearded men, calling them santos (saints), while men marched with signs that read, "Gracias, Fidel!" (Thank you, Fidel!)

A triumphant Castro rides into Havana in 1959 atop a military jeep. He is joined by members of his Rebel Army and many grateful supporters.

CASTRO WAS LOOKING FOR MY FATHER AND A LOT OF OTHER BATISTA PEOPLE. IT WAS JUST VERY TERRIFYING.

—Tamahra Calzadilla

The Cubans knew that a new page had turned in their history. Castro seemed to be a modern version of José Martí, the nineteenth-century hero of independence. Castro's larger-than-life personality sparked popular support for the revolution. When he spoke to cheering crowds on January 9, 1959, two doves suddenly appeared, and one landed on his left shoulder. This event was seen as a symbol of a new era.

MANY PEOPLE ARE INTERESTED IN LEARNING ABOUT THEIR FAMILY'S HISTORY. THIS STUDY IS CALLED GENEALOGY. IF YOU'D LIKE TO LEARN ABOUT YOUR OWN GENEALOGY AND HOW YOUR ANCESTORS CAME TO AMERICA, VISIT WWW.INAMERICABOOKS.COM FOR TIPS AND LINKS TO HELP GET YOU STARTED. THERE YOU'LL ALSO FIND TIPS ON RESEARCHING NAMES IN YOUR FAMILY HISTORY.

Dramatic Changes

It was indeed a new era, but for many Cubans, it was not a joyous one. Following Castro's triumph, he moved quickly to cement his power. Several members of Batista's regime were put on trial and jailed. Although Castro initially refused any kind of official role in his new government, he soon named himself prime minister.

Dramatic changes started to take place in Cuba. In May 1959, the government passed a land reform law, breaking up estates larger than one thousand acres. The government seized any properties over this size and turned them into collective (government-run) farms or gave the land to poor peasants. Many foreign-owned companies were nationalized, or taken over by the Cuban government. As opposition to his power mounted, Castro silenced his critics by abolishing freedom of the press in May 1960.

Castro's rise to power provoked several waves of emigration, sometimes referred to as the great migration. Cubans who opposed the revolution or gradually became disillusioned with it chose to leave the island. They sought refuge and freedom in their northern neighbor, the United States.

2 Exiles and Immigrants

During the first half of the twentieth century, a steady flow of immigrants had come from Cuba to the United States each year, but the Cuban American community was still fairly small. In 1959, when Castro came to power, about 120,000 Cubans were living in the United States. Many more came after 1959.

The Golden Exiles

In the first six months of 1959, more than 26,000 Cubans moved to the United States. The first people to flee Cuba after the revolution were those who supported Batista, known as *batistianos*. They feared for their lives, since many of Batista's associates had already faced Castro's firing squads. Others who took flight to the United States were members of Cuba's upper classes: business executives, sugar mill owners, representatives of foreign companies, and other professionals with close ties to the

United States. They had lost their property and social status, and they were afraid of more changes to come.

Scholars, writers, and other intellectuals were also among the early exiles. Anyone who expressed any criticism of the government faced years in jail or worse. Many intellectuals left Cuba to avoid imprisonment and to maintain their freedom to express themselves.

Most of the exiles settled in Miami, Florida. Miami was appealing in a number of ways. It was close to home, just a forty-five-minute plane trip from Cuba. The climate in South Florida reminded them of Cuba. Many upper-class Cubans were already familiar with the United States, since they had spent time there on vacations or business trips. Many of them had ties to the United States or knew someone who was already living in Florida.

Of all U.S. cities, Miami, Florida (below), *has drawn the most Cuban immigrants. The climate reminds them of home, and they have created vibrant communities in their new city.*

The Revolution brought an abrupt change to my life. Everything that I had been taught and stood for changed. Castro appeared on television and reported, "Last night we passed a law and everybody who doesn't agree with it will be put into prison." I knew then I would have to leave or they would kill me.

—Irma de Leon

This first wave of immigrants became known as the Golden Exiles because of their wealth and high social status. Although many were forced to leave their money and possessions behind in Cuba, they brought with them skills, education, contacts, and families. These resources helped them get established in the United States. The immigrants learned English, found jobs, and started businesses.

The early Cuban exiles organized associations called *municipios en exilio* (municipalities in exile) to help other new arrivals from the island adjust to life in the United States. Named after townships in Cuba, each municipio served immigrants who came from the township it was named for. The municipios provided a variety of services, such as English classes, job information, and emergency aid. They were also a way for people to keep in touch with old colleagues and friends from the island, to celebrate holidays together, and to promote Cuban culture and political aims.

Even as the Golden Exiles adjusted to life in the United States, they assumed they would return to Cuba. They believed that their stay in the United States would be short. Many celebrated their first Christmas in Miami with a traditional pot roast and anticipated enjoying the same meal the following year with family and friends back in Cuba.

Meanwhile, Cuba's relationship with the United States was quickly

deteriorating. After negotiating to buy oil from the Soviet Union in 1960, Castro asked three U.S. oil companies to process the oil at their Cuban refineries. But the United States was involved in a conflict with the Soviet Union known as the Cold War. It was fought with economic and political actions rather than weapons. The U.S. companies refused to process Soviet oil, and the United States announced that it would no longer buy Cuban sugar, a move that would damage Cuba's economy. Castro fought back by taking over U.S.-owned sugar mills, telephone companies, and electric companies in Cuba.

Tensions continued to increase over the course of the year. In mid-October, U.S. president Dwight Eisenhower put an embargo on Cuban products, meaning the United States would not trade (buy or sell goods) with Cuba. Eisenhower hoped that Cubans would blame their new government for shortages of food and goods and turn against Castro.

TO LEARN MORE ABOUT FIDEL CASTRO AND HOW HIS RISE TO POWER AFFECTED CUBA'S RELATIONSHIP WITH THE UNITED STATES, VISIT WWW.INAMERICABOOKS.COM FOR LINKS.

Castro retaliated by taking over all U.S. private enterprises in Cuba, including banks, the remaining sugar mills, and other large industries. In 1961 the United States cut off formal relations with Cuba. Castro turned to the Soviet Union for military and economic aid. The Soviets agreed to buy one million tons of Cuban sugar each year, loan the Cuban government $100 million, and sell weapons, raw materials, and manufactured goods to Cuba. Soon the Soviet Union replaced the United States as Cuba's most important trading partner.

Castro's government actively campaigned against U.S. values in favor of Cuban ones. At Christmas, images of Santa Claus were banned and replaced by images of Don Feliciano, a typical Cuban farmer wearing a guayabera, or tropical shirt, and a straw hat. The chant "Cuba sí, Yanquis no!" (Yes to Cuba, no to Yankees! [Americans]) was broadcast repeatedly over Cuban radio stations.

In April 1961, Castro announced that the Cuban revolution was a socialist one. Cuban society had previously been based on private enterprise, in which private individuals are free to own land and businesses and operate them for a profit. Under socialism, Cubans were expected to work for society as a whole, rather than for their own benefit. They were asked to put collective or group values first and personal gain second. The economy was restructured, so that the government controlled factories, farms, and other businesses.

When Castro first took over, he had declared that Cuba would not be a Communist country like the Soviet Union. But in the eyes of the world, his form of socialism looked just like Communism.

The Bay of Pigs

As Castro was creating a socialist state, Cuban exiles living in the United States were plotting his overthrow. In April 1961, a group of about 1,400 Cuban exiles, backed by the U.S. government, landed in military boats at the Bay of Pigs in southern Cuba. The exiles, calling themselves Brigade 2506, planned to invade the country

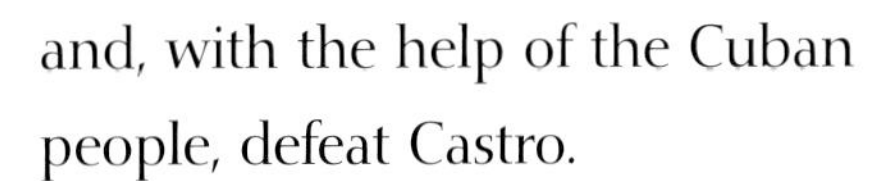

and, with the help of the Cuban people, defeat Castro.

The invasion was a disaster. Castro had been tipped off about the plan, and twenty thousand troops were waiting to confront the exiles. Only fifty Cubans joined the brigade once it hit the beaches. Castro's troops captured almost everyone in the brigade, ending the exiles' dreams of liberation.

After the Bay of Pigs incident, a second wave of Cuban migration took place, from April 1961 to October 1962. This time it was the middle class that left. Businesspeople, lawyers, doctors, teachers, skilled workers, and other middle-class citizens were convinced that after the failure of the U.S.-led invasion, they had no future in Cuba. And they no longer had faith in Cuba's political system. Castro had outlawed free elections. He declared himself a Marxist-Leninist, referring to the founders of Communism, German philosopher Karl Marx and Soviet leader Vladimir Lenin. Only one political party, the Communist Party, was allowed in Cuba. People who opposed Castro's regime were put in jail. By 1961 as many as ten thousand political prisoners were being held in Cuba.

Many Cubans also feared for their children's welfare. Rumors circulated that children might be

When I emotionally turned the page, was after the Bay of Pigs. When those men came back . . . I said: "This is it; we have done what was expected of us to recover Cuba." . . . So, at that point, I said to myself: "I think this country [the United States] has a lot to offer. I'm not going to forget my country of origin, but I'm here and I'm gonna represent Cuba and act in the most dignified and in the most successful way that I can to represent my country of origin."

—María Elena Toraño

sent to the Soviet Union to be educated or that parents would lose their legal rights to make decisions about their children. As a result, thousands of Cuban children between the ages of six and sixteen were sent to the United States under the guardianship of the Catholic Church in Miami.

No one knew if we would ever see one another again, and although everyone hoped that the Americans would overthrow Fidel, it never happened. Meanwhile, my memory returns me to the terrifying face of my mother, crying out with a desperate scream, desperate but silent, the scream that I still carry inside me.

—Flora González Mandri, part of Operation Peter Pan

By 1962 more than 150,000 Cubans had left their homeland. The U.S. government established the Cuban Refugee Program to help the exiles adjust to their new surroundings. Between 1961 and 1971, the U.S. government spent more than $730 million on aid programs for Cuban immigrants. The help included job training, English language instruction, medical care, financial assistance for housing, food stamps, cash, and low-cost loans for college.

The U.S. government encouraged Cuban immigration, hoping it would hurt Castro by draining Cuba of its best and brightest citizens. The exodus also showed the world that Cubans were unhappy with Communism. Unlike immigrants from other countries, who needed permission to enter the United States, all Cubans were welcomed, whether or not they had official documents. They were assumed to be refugees—people fleeing a country for fear of punishment or danger—and were given benefits.

Operation Peter Pan

Under Operation Pedro Pan (Peter Pan), more than fourteen thousand Cuban children—alone, without their parents—boarded planes and left Cuba between 1960 and 1962. The Catholic Church and other groups organized the program out of fear that Cuban children were in danger of being sent to the Soviet Union and trained in Communist teachings.

The Cuban children stayed in temporary shelters and camps in southern Florida until they were adopted by American families or reunited with their parents. Life in the camps—and the experience of being uprooted and thrust into a new culture and language—was wrenching for these children. Many of them never saw their families again. Despite the difficulties, many of the Peter Pan children *(above)* went on to become successful businesspeople and professionals.

Although some Cuban families moved to other states, the majority chose to live in Florida. The U.S. government, concerned about the impact that a large influx of Spanish-speaking residents would have in South Florida, started a resettlement program to entice Cuban immigrants to move to other states. Cuban exiles were offered job assistance, free transportation, and a modest sum of cash if they were willing to live and work away from the Miami area.

These efforts, as well as job opportunities, led many Cubans to big cities such as New York, Chicago, and Los Angeles. Outside of Miami, the largest number of Cuban immigrants went to New York, which already had a large Cuban population. Many Cubans also settled in New Jersey.

> EVERY SINGLE UNCLE THAT HAD LEFT CUBA CAME TO LIVE IN THIS APARTMENT IN THE BRONX. WE WERE THIRTEEN PEOPLE LIVING IN THIS APARTMENT WITH ROACHES.
>
> *—Rosa Vazquez*

REFUGEES IN RAFTS

In October 1962, U.S. military spy planes sighted Soviet missile launching sites in Cuba. The missiles would be capable of sending nuclear warheads to the United States. President John F. Kennedy ordered a naval blockade, surrounding Cuba with warships to prevent Soviet missiles from being delivered to the island. In what became known as the Cuban missile crisis, President Kennedy and Soviet leader Nikita Khrushchev negotiated through the standoff as Americans and Cubans lived through dangerous days under the threat of nuclear destruction.

RESETTLING THE REFUGEES

To ease the impact that thousands of Cuban refugees would have on South Florida's social agencies and economy, in 1962 the U.S. government started a resettlement program to encourage Cubans to move to other parts of the country. More than 250,000 Cuban refugees took the offer. Many were professionals who saw better prospects elsewhere.

As one Cuban American recalled, "My father could not get a job in Miami, because if you were Cuban in the early 1960s, you could not get a job here, you could not rent a house, you could hardly get a telephone without a substantial deposit. So, for lack of opportunities for my father, we left Miami and ended up in Long Island, New York, and that's where I grew up."

The largest number of resettled Cubans, 80,483, went to New York. Another 58,791 went to New Jersey. A few ended up in places with no Cuban community, such as North Dakota and Maine, and one lone Cuban went to Alaska. The Cubans left Miami with mixed feelings, but they were determined to carve out a new life.

In the long run, however, many of the resettled Cubans returned to Florida. They felt more comfortable in a place that was more like home, where other Cubans lived, the weather was balmy, and they could find the food and music they enjoyed.

The crisis was settled when the Soviets agreed to withdraw the missiles and dismantle their bases in Cuba. In exchange, the United States agreed not to invade the island. Feeling left out of this crucial agreement, a raging Fidel Castro refused to allow inspection

of Cuban territory to determine whether the missiles had been removed. U.S. air inspections revealed that they were being removed, however, and the naval blockade of Cuba was lifted.

Cuban migration patterns changed after the missile crisis, when Castro canceled all regular flights from Cuba to the United States. The only Cubans who were allowed to leave for the United States were prisoners who had been captured during the Bay of Pigs invasion and their relatives. Castro agreed to release the prisoners in exchange for much-needed medicine and food. Although Cuban emigration slowed down, it did not stop altogether. People continued to flee the island in boats and on makeshift rafts built out of tires. By 1965 another thirty-five thousand Cubans had made their way to the United States.

A small wooden boat in Key West, Florida, serves as a memorial to the thousands of Cubans who risked their lives in such crafts to escape oppression in their homeland.

1962
CUBAN REFUGEE BOATS
DEDICATED TO THOSE MEN WOMEN AND CHILDREN WHO RISKED DEATH FOR FREEDOM.

From 1962 to 1965, the composition of exile groups also shifted as discontent spread among poor and working-class Cubans as well as middle-class citizens. Part of their unhappiness stemmed from two unpopular measures passed in 1962 and 1963: a food rationing system, which provided a guaranteed but limited amount of food for each family, and forced military service for young men. Office and factory

workers, farmers, and fishers began to leave, along with professionals who had not fled earlier.

By the mid-1960s, many Cubans in the United States realized they were in their new country to stay. They still dreamed of Cuba, spoke Spanish, and cooked black beans and rice, a traditional Cuban dish. But they forged new lives in the United States. Many Cubans gave up their hope of defeating Castro. Instead, they began to focus their efforts on home, business, and community.

In Miami the exiles settled in an area known as Little Havana. In this neighborhood, everyone spoke Spanish, Cubans owned the shops and businesses, and the scent of Cuban foods drifted in the air. In Little Havana, Cuban Americans reproduced the society they had left behind in Cuba.

The Cuban exiles also kept up their traditions at home. Family remained the cornerstone of life, and extended families often lived together or near each other. They

Cuban markets in Little Havana carry all the comforts of home. By creating a little piece of Cuba in Miami, many Cuban immigrants found it easier to adjust to life in the United States.

gathered frequently for meals, enjoying favorite Cuban foods such as rice and beans, fried plantains, and chicken with rice. They celebrated Christmas Eve with the traditional roast pig. A common toast at celebrations was "Next year in Cuba," keeping alive the dream of returning to the island.

Most Americans welcomed the early Cuban exiles. Cubans were seen as having similar values, such as a belief in hard work, education, and a desire for freedom. The American press published many reports of "Cuban success stories" or "those amazing Cubans."

Freedom Flights

The next wave of Cuban migration began in the fall of 1965, when Castro announced a surprising change in emigration policy. He declared that anyone wishing to go to the United States could do so. His goal was to reunite families who were separated. Hundreds of Cubans in Miami sailed in private boats to the small Cuban port city of Camarioca in Mantanzas Province. There, they picked up their relatives and brought them back to the United States. This chaotic situation lasted for two months, until the U.S. and Cuban governments finally arranged for an orderly "air bridge," a series of flights that began in December 1965.

From 1965 to 1973, official Freedom Flights left the Varadero airport in Mantanzas, bringing 300,000 Cubans to Miami. Priority was given to relatives of Cubans already living in the United States. This wave of immigrants included shopkeepers, craftspeople, and other service workers. Some people were not allowed to leave, including young men of military age (fifteen to twenty-six), professionals such as doctors and lawyers, and other skilled workers.

Many of the immigrants came to the United States seeking to improve their standard of living. Food and household goods had become increasingly scarce in Cuba. Under Castro's socialist policies, farms and businesses had little incentive to do well. Although

Cubans disembark from an official Freedom Flight in the late 1960s.

Castro's regime had developed many social welfare programs, such as free education, health care, and day care for children, the state-run economy was suffering from poor management and bad decisions.

Cubans who declared their intention to emigrate were denounced as enemies of the revolution. They were forced from their jobs and even their homes. It often took years to receive a visa to exit the country. During that time, emigrants faced countless ordeals and often had to depend on relatives or friends for their survival.

To discover some of the many stories of Cubans migrating to the United States, Visit www.inamericabooks.com for links.

When the Freedom Flight immigrants arrived in the United States, they were welcomed and helped by the Cuban communities established by the earlier immigrants. The Golden Exiles had prospered in

Florida and elsewhere. By the end of the 1970s, more than one-third of Miami's businesses were owned by Cuban immigrants. These businesses included shops of all sorts, restaurants, banks, supermarkets, law firms, and doctors' and dentists' offices. New arrivals from Cuba found jobs at these companies, and they soon began to start their own businesses.

Outside the Cuban community, however, the welcome wasn't always so warm. As more and more exiles arrived in Miami, some Anglos (white Americans) showed hostility toward the newcomers. Cuban American banker Luis Botifoll recalled, "Some people resented our presence here because we [spoke] a different language, we were talking too loud, we didn't have enough money, and, when we rented an apartment, a two-room apartment, maybe seven or eight relatives would move in."

[Cubans in the United States] were more than willing to overwork themselves to death to give a chance to the young, and also to make sure that the young felt proud of their Cuban heritage.

—Mercedes Sandoval

When darker-skinned Cubans began moving into white neighborhoods, they met with resistance. Juan Manuel Alonso, who left Cuba at the age of fourteen with his family as part of the Freedom Flights, remembered, "As a kid, it seemed to me that Miami was a big swamp filled with mosquitoes; among my first impressions were seeing segregated water fountains for Whites and Blacks and encountering rental signs that read 'No Blacks, No Dogs, No Cubans.'"

Some white residents of Miami chose to move to the suburbs rather than live near people of a different race. Many Cuban

Not all Americans were hostile toward the new Cuban immigrants of the 1970s. Some people showed their support for Cubans by displaying bumper stickers such as the one above, which means "yes to Cuba."

Americans bristled at a bumper sticker that became popular in Florida in the 1970s. It said, "Will the last American leaving Miami, please bring the flag?" Cuban Americans retorted with a bumper sticker of their own: "Will the last bigot leaving Miami, please see me for gas money."

The Revolution Betrayed

Back in Cuba, the dream of the revolution was fading into a nightmare. The economy was failing, and the hardships of daily life caused many Cubans to lose faith in the revolution. Adequate housing was hard to find. Newlywed couples often continued living with their parents, and many houses were split into makeshift apartments to house relatives in need. Castro's strict rationing

system was supposed to ensure that everyone had enough to eat, but severe food shortages left people hungry and desperate.

Castro adopted the Soviet model of Communism in 1971. Che Guevara, Castro's fellow revolutionary, disagreed with Castro's embrace of Soviet-style Communism. Guevara left Cuba for a doomed attempt to start a revolution in Bolivia. His tragic death in the ragged hills of Bolivia made Che a legendary figure throughout Latin America.

Ordinary people who disagreed with Fidel's political system were treated harshly. Enrique Patterson recalled what happened when he publicly criticized Castro in Cuba: "From that time forward I was labeled as having 'ideological problems' and was punished for my disobedience. Not only was I let go from every position I had, but I was eliminated as a possible candidate to receive a scholarship to study in Germany and banned from traveling anywhere outside of Cuba. At one point, when I worked at a print shop, I was reprimanded for not wearing socks to work."

Castro also cracked down in the cultural sphere. Cuban writers and artists were not allowed to express their views, and the works of foreign authors were banned. Heberto Padilla, considered one of Cuba's greatest poets, was jailed for criticizing the revolution in his poem "Out of the Game." The only accepted literary works were those that idealized the revolution and glossed over the many hardships of daily life in Cuba.

The Dialogue

The icy divide between Cuba and the United States after Castro's revolution began to crack open a bit in December 1977, when a group of young, college-educated Cuban Americans traveled to Cuba. Calling themselves the Antonio Maceo Brigade, after a general in the Cuban wars of independence, these idealistic young men and women were influenced by the American civil rights movement and demonstrations against the Vietnam War (1957–1975). Brigade members toured the island, worked side by side with Cuban laborers at a construction site outside Havana, and met high-ranking government officials, including Fidel Castro himself. The visitors were hailed in Cuba as fellow revolutionaries.

Then, in late 1978, Castro and members of his government met with representatives of the Cuban community in the United States, Spain, and Mexico. Known as el Diálogo, or the Dialogue, the talks resulted in the release of people who had been imprisoned in Cuba because of their political views. In addition, Castro allowed exiles to return regularly to Cuba to visit their families.

In the United States, the Dialogue divided the Cuban American community into two camps—those who supported the Dialogue and those who opposed it. Some of the opponents carried out terrorist acts against its participants. One of the original members of the Antonio Maceo Brigade was gunned down in Puerto Rico in April 1979, and a Dialogue participant was shot in New Jersey in November of that year.

THE MARIEL BOATLIFT

Growing discontent in Cuba came to a head in 1980. On April 1, a dozen Cubans broke into the Peruvian Embassy in Havana and asked for political asylum—safe passage out of Cuba. They knew that the Peruvian government had granted asylum to other Cubans who had entered the embassy, allowing them to move to Peru. When the Peruvian ambassador refused to turn over the gate-crashers to the Cuban police, Castro tried to provoke a crisis for the ambassador. He announced that the embassy was open to any Cubans who wished to leave.

Word spread that the gates were open, and within a few days, hundreds of people flocked to the embassy. Waiting without food, water, or public toilets, the crowd grew to more than ten thousand people. Castro realized he had a problem that was rapidly spinning out of control. He decided to allow people to leave from Mariel, a small port city about twenty miles from Havana. This was the opportunity that many disgruntled and weary Cubans had been waiting for.

Castro saw it as a way to rid the island of anyone who opposed his regime. He also seized the opportunity to cast out citizens he viewed as undesirable, including criminals, mentally ill people, and homosexuals. Many of these "social undesirables" were sent to sea whether they wanted to leave or not. Writer Reinaldo Arenas left Cuba unexpectedly when a government official knocked at his door with the order to kick out all gay people.

WORMS AND SCUM

Since the early days of his regime, Fidel Castro has referred to anyone who left Cuba or wanted to leave as *gusanos*, or "worms." When Castro announced that Cubans were free to leave the country from the port of Mariel, he had a new name for those he considered traitors—*escoria*, or "scum."

Hundreds of Cubans in Miami sailed to Mariel harbor to pick up their relatives. Many Cuban Americans managed to bring their relatives back, but others had to take whomever the angry Cuban officials dumped in their boats. The exodus, known as the Mariel Boatlift, continued for five months. By the time Castro finally suspended it in September 1980, nearly 125,000 Cubans had made their way to the United States.

In the United States, President Jimmy Carter did not quite know how to handle the flood of immigrants. Fortunately, Cuban American groups raised funds to help the refugees. Some went to temporary shelters, tent cities, and parks in Miami. Others were housed and fed at Fort Walton Beach, a city in the Florida Panhandle at the northwestern edge of the state. Many refugees were transported to Fort Chaffee, an army base in Arkansas, where they were met by hostile local residents who fired shots at them. Cut off, imprisoned, and unsure of their fate, some of the Cuban refugees at Fort Chaffee broke out in riots.

The U.S. media painted a negative picture of the Marielitos, as the refugees were known, portraying them as criminals and social misfits. In truth, of the 125,000 Cubans who left through

Hundreds of Marielitos celebrate their arrival in the United States in 1980.

Mariel, only about 1 percent turned out to be criminals by U.S. standards. The majority of Marielitos were blue-collar workers, and a few were professionals such as teachers, accountants, and nurses. Whereas earlier waves of Cuban immigrants had arrived in family groups, most Marielitos were young, single men.

In Miami the refugees faced many obstacles. Jobs were scarce, because the United States was in a period of economic recession, or lowered business activity. Black Marielitos faced racial discrimination, as well as the prejudices of their fellow Cubans. The refugees' attitudes about work were more relaxed than those of previous Cuban immigrants. Cuba's socialist system provided little incentive to work hard, since individuals could not profit from their work. This attitude went against the prevailing Cuban American ethic, which stressed hard work and financial success. As a

result, many Marielitos struggled to find a place in the fast-paced, capitalist society of the United States.

Following the Mariel exodus, tensions rose between Cubans and Miami's other ethnic groups. Voters in Dade County (where Miami is located) overturned an ordinance that required county documents to be printed in both English and Spanish, and the county adopted English as its only official language. Friction was especially high between Cuban and non-Cuban blacks. U.S.-born blacks resented the Marielitos because Afro-Cubans often found it easier than African Americans to get jobs.

In 1981 a group of prominent Cuban American businesspeople founded the Cuban American National Foundation. Led by millionaire Jorge Mas Canosa, the group was dedicated to bringing democracy to Cuba by influencing U.S. foreign policy. Headquartered in Washington, D.C., the foundation became the most powerful force in Cuban American politics.

As Cuban Americans' economic and political power grew, they also distinguished themselves in the arts. Many artists and writers were among the Mariel refugees, and after the boatlift, Cuban communities across the United States experienced a cultural awakening. Cuban American writers such as Oscar Hijuelos reached a wide U.S. audience. Events such as the Miami Film Festival, the Calle Ocho Festival, and the Miami Carnival, along with a flowering of Cuban American theater and music performances, kept Cuban culture thriving in the United States.

IT TOOK US A LONG TIME TO GET USED TO EVEN THE MOST BASIC FREEDOMS THAT EVERY AMERICAN TAKES FOR GRANTED, SUCH AS THE IDEA THAT WE COULD TRAVEL WHEREVER WE WANTED WITHOUT ASKING FOR PERMISSION, OR THAT WE COULD ACTUALLY MAKE DECISIONS FOR OURSELVES.

—Effrain J. Ferrer and Vivan de la Incera

Costumed dancers perform during a Cuban festival in Little Havana. Maintaining their cultural traditions is important to Cuban Americans and helps them feel connected to the homeland many still hope to return to someday.

While many Cuban Americans were enjoying success in the United States, Cubans themselves were still struggling, especially during the early 1990s. Between 1989 and 1991, the Communist government of the Soviet Union collapsed, and the nation broke into separate republics. Communist regimes in other Eastern European countries were also overthrown.

The breakup of the Soviet Union had a devastating effect on Cuba's economy. Cuba lost its most important trading partner and billions of dollars a year in assistance. With no place to sell their products and nowhere to get the raw materials they needed, many Cuban factories shut down. In 1990 Castro put into place a policy called the Special Period in Peacetime, which tightened rations on food and other goods and reduced energy consumption. Extreme shortages of food and everyday necessities caused some of the worst hardships Cubans had ever faced.

As political repression and food shortages worsened, more Cubans became desperate to leave the island. But getting out wasn't easy. During the early 1990s, Castro allowed only a few thousand Cubans to emigrate from Cuba to

the United States each year. For most people, the only way to reach the United States was by crossing the Straits of Florida by boat, a dangerous trip that many attempted in small handmade rafts.

Some Cubans staged more dramatic escapes. In 1991 Orestes Lorenzo, an officer in the Cuban air force, flew his military jet to Florida, where he was given asylum. He made headlines the following year when he rescued his wife and children by flying an old airplane and landing on a highway in the Cuban countryside. In the spring of 1992, another family attempted to flee Cuba in a helicopter used for spraying crops, but they crashed and died.

In response to the flood of rafters heading across the Straits of Florida, a Cuban exile named José Basulto founded Brothers to the Rescue in 1991. The group's volunteer members flew small planes between Havana and Miami, helping rafters in trouble.

The Balseros

In the summer of 1994, small groups of Cubans trying to leave the country hijacked several passenger ferries operating off the coast of Havana and forced the boats to go to Miami. As word of the hijackings spread, thousands of Cubans gathered each morning near the ferries, hoping to hitch a ride on the next hijacked vessel. When the police tried to disband the crowd on August 5, a huge riot broke out. Hundreds of Cubans attacked the police and shouted out their opposition to Castro's regime.

Castro responded to the crisis as he had in the past, by saying that people who wanted to leave Cuba were free to do so. He hoped to create problems for U.S. president Bill Clinton and force him to lift the U.S. trade embargo against Cuba. Clinton refused to end the embargo. He also stated that Cuban Americans would be prevented from sailing to Cuba to pick up friends and relatives. The president hoped to avoid another flood of refugees like the Marielitos.

Within days, however, tens of thousands of Cubans set to sea in makeshift boats and rafts. The refugees tried to cross the ninety-mile-wide waterway with anything they could find that would float—plywood, inner tubes, Styrofoam cups melted together, or empty oil drums tied together. One group even tried to cross the Florida Straits by attaching oil drums and a propeller to a 1951 Chevrolet truck, converting it into a pontoon (a flat-bottomed boat).

Many of the rafts were unsafe and unseaworthy. As a result, many

Many Cubans have resorted to extreme measures in their eagerness to flee Castro's regime. This group of emigrants converted an old Chevy into a pontoon, but they were returned to Cuba by the U.S. Coast Guard.

WE WERE THE LAST PEOPLE TO GET ON THIS BOAT. . . . IT WAS JUST A FISHING BOAT, BUILT TO HOLD ABOUT 50 PEOPLE, BUT NOT FOR TRAVELING ACROSS THE OCEAN. THERE WERE MANY MORE PEOPLE ON THIS BOAT ON THAT TRIP. HOLDING ONTO THE SAILS, ON TOP OF THE ROOF OF THE CABIN, HOLDING ONTO THE SIDES OF THE BOAT.

—Rolando (last name unknown)

rafters, or *balseros*, as they are called in Spanish, drowned. No one is sure how many people died at sea, but the number is thought to be in the thousands.

The rafter migration was the largest exodus of Cubans since the Mariel boatlift. By mid-September more than thirty-two thousand Cubans had made it to the United States or been picked up by the U.S. Coast Guard. As more and more balseros took to the water, the U.S. government tried to stop the flood. President Clinton was already dealing with a crisis of refugees coming from Haiti, another troubled Caribbean nation. The U.S. government built a huge refugee camp at the U.S. naval base at Guantánamo Bay, Cuba, and resettled many Cuban and Haitian refugees there. Clinton announced that any balseros picked up by the U.S. Coast Guard would be sent to Guantánamo or to other Latin American countries.

Eventually most of the Cubans at the refugee camp were allowed to enter the United States. But in 1994, the U.S. government changed its long-standing policy toward Cuban immigrants. Since Castro's revolution, Cubans who had fled the island had been guaranteed asylum in the United States. In September 1994 and May 1995, the United States and Cuba signed new joint agreements on immigration.

Under the new policy, the United States would no longer give automatic asylum to Cuban refugees, but it would admit twenty thousand legal immigrants from Cuba each year. In turn, Castro agreed to return to his former policy of preventing Cubans from

leaving without permission. Demand for exit visas was far greater than the number of legal immigrants allowed to come, however.

Another U.S. law allowed any Cuban who reached U.S. soil to remain as a lawful, permanent resident. As a result, thousands of Cuban rafters continued to cross the shark-infested waters between Cuba and Florida. In what was known as the "wet-foot, dry-foot" policy, Cubans who were caught in the water (wet foot) by the U.S. Coast Guard were returned, or repatriated, to Cuba, while those who made it to U.S. soil (dry foot) were allowed to stay.

In February 1996, the Cuban military shot down two U.S. civilian aircraft piloted by members of Brothers to the Rescue. Four Cuban Americans died in the incident. In retaliation, the U.S. Congress called for President Bill Clinton to sign the Helms-Burton Act into law. The law tightened the trade embargo even more. U.S. lawmakers hoped the embargo would force Cuba's economy to collapse and spur the end of Castro's regime. Opponents in the United States and around the world said the embargo, rather than achieving the stated goal, only caused suffering among the Cuban people.

Elián González

In November 1999, two fishers from the United States rescued Elián González, a six-year-old Cuban boy, in the Atlantic Ocean off the coast of Florida. Elián and his mother had fled Cuba in a small, poorly made boat along with about a dozen other people. The boy's mother and most of the other rafters drowned when the boat sank. Elián clung to an inner tube for two days before he was found. Family members in Miami were determined to keep the boy, but his father, who lived in Cuba, wanted him back.

The Cuban American community rallied behind Elián's Miami relatives. Led by Lincoln Diaz-Balart, a congressperson from

Florida, Cuban Americans held demonstrations, protests, candlelight vigils, and press conferences. Most other Americans felt that Elián belonged with his father. The controversy divided Miami residents and led to sharp criticism of Cuban Americans by non-Cuban Americans in Florida and elsewhere.

After several months of legal battles and daily media coverage, President Clinton sent federal officers to remove Elián from his relatives' home by force. The boy was reunited with his father, and they returned to Cuba. Thousands of Cuban Americans were united by profound grief and outrage. They saw Elián as a symbol of their own struggle to find freedom in the United States. After the raid in which federal officials seized the boy, Cuban Americans demonstrated in the streets. Some of the protests turned violent. But a week later, about 100,000 Cuban Americans gathered in a peaceful protest.

Elián embraces his father after the two were reunited at Andrews Air Force Base in Maryland in April 2000.

3

Little Havana and Beyond

Cuban Americans are united by a strong sense of Cubanidad, or cultural identity. The common bonds of language and culture have contributed to the stability of the Cuban community in the United States. Cuban Americans have made important contributions in business, the arts, entertainment, sports, and politics. In just one generation, Cuban Americans have achieved a standard of living comparable to the U.S. norm.

Cuban Communities

Although Cuban Americans can be found throughout the United States, Miami remains the heart and soul of the community. More than 60 percent of Cuban Americans live in Florida, mainly in Dade County, where Miami is located. They continue to appreciate Florida's climate, the chance to live near relatives, and the sense of community they find in South Florida.

Miami's Little Havana is the historical and geographical center of the Cuban community in the United States. At the heart of Little Havana is Calle Ocho, or Southwest Eighth Street, which is lined with Cuban shops, coffeehouses, bakeries, banks, car dealerships, and restaurants. In Domino Park, older men gather daily to play dominoes and checkers. They discuss politics in between puffs of cigars that are almost as good as the ones back in Cuba.

Popular Little Havana restaurants such as La Carreta and Versailles serve typical Cuban meals such as a plate of roast pork, rice and black beans, and fried plantains, or *arroz con pollo* (chicken and rice). Street vendors pour *café cubano*—dark, sweet espresso

Friends gather in Little Havana's Domino Park for a game of dominoes.

Many states boast Cuban eateries. Victor's 1959 Café in Minneapolis, Minnesota, offers café con leche *(coffee with milk) and other tastes of Cuba.*

coffee—and sell snacks, such as Cuban sandwiches and empanandas, meat- or fruit-filled turnovers.

Small grocery stores, or bodegas, carry Cuban fruits and vegetables, including plantains and the starchy, tropical root vegetables yucca (*yuca* in Spanish), boniato, and malanga. Specialty stores called botanicas sell products used by followers of Santeria. Botanicas sell medicinal herbs and potions, ornaments, statues, and other objects used in religious rituals.

Besides Domino Park, another important gathering spot is Cuban Memorial Boulevard, on Thirteenth Avenue off Calle Ocho. This parkway contains a series of monuments honoring the history and culture of Cuba. It also serves as a place for community

WHEN CUBANS GATHER FOR CAFÉ, IT ALWAYS COMES WITH A LOT OF CONVERSATION, DEBATE, AND HUMOR.

—"Three Guys from Miami" (Raúl Musibay, Glenn Lindgren, Jorge Castillo)

gatherings, celebrations, and political demonstrations.

Little Havana is changing, as large numbers of immigrants from other Latin American nations move to Miami. For example, the area previously known as Northeast Little Havana has come to be called Little Managua because of the influx of people from Nicaragua. (Managua is the capital of Nicaragua.) Other immigrant groups have brought their own traditions and foods to Little Havana. Almost every restaurant in the area serves *tres leches* (three milks) cake, a Nicaraguan dessert.

While the Little Havana section of Miami remains the center of the Cuban American population, many Cubans have moved to the city's wealthier neighborhoods. Many Cubans live in suburban areas near Miami, including Hialeah, Kendall, and Miami Lakes, and in the city of Tampa, on Florida's west coast. Significant Cuban American communities also are found in New York, New Jersey, Illinois, and California.

I have now spent most of my life in South Florida, where I enjoy a lifestyle that reminds me of the Cuba I once left. I can walk to the corner cafeteria and savor an aromatic café cubano, go to the neighborhood bookstore and browse through any book, or invite friends to my home and engage in a lively political discussion. These are a few of the simple things most of my brothers and sisters on the island can no longer do; there, coffee is rationed, books are censored, and the . . . secret police can burst into any gathering unannounced.

—Miguel Gonzalez-Pando

Success Stories

Starting with the Golden Exiles and continuing through successive waves of immigration, Cubans who settled in the United States have established an outstanding record of economic success. Even though Cuban Americans make up less than 5 percent of the Hispanic population in the United States, they own nearly 30 percent of Hispanic-owned businesses. Fewer Cuban Americans live in poverty compared to other Hispanic groups.

Bilingual Education

Cuban Americans helped pioneer the field of bilingual education. As the first wave of Cuban exiles arrived in Dade County, Florida, in the early 1960s, a group of political activists, psychologists, and educators began to question the traditional way of teaching immigrant students—placing them in regular classes taught in English only. Educators believed that Hispanic children who were taught in English were being forced to abandon their own cultures.

To overcome this problem, teachers included Hispanic history and culture in their lessons. Children could learn math, science, and social studies in Spanish while taking English as a second language. Gradually, as their English improved, the students took all classes in English.

In 1963 the Dade County schools started the first completely bilingual program in grades one through three at the Coral Way School in Miami. The federal government funded bilingual education in Dade County throughout the 1960s. In 1980, however, supporters of English-only teaching helped get rid of public funding for bilingual education.

FIND LINKS FOR MORE INFORMATION ABOUT THE MANY WAYS THAT PEOPLE OF CUBAN HERITAGE CONTRIBUTE TO LIFE IN AMERICA AT WWW.INAMERICABOOKS.COM.

Many of the early Cuban exiles were well educated and highly skilled. They created a strong community and comfortable life in their new home. Even though the Mariel refugees tended to be poorer than earlier Cuban immigrants, within a decade, most of the Marielitos had proven to be just as successful in learning English, finding jobs, and building businesses as the earlier Cuban immigrants.

The most recent immigrants have tended to be well educated, professional, and motivated, and they

WE LOST EVERYTHING WE POSSESSED IN CUBA, BUT THE ONE THING THAT CASTRO COULD NEVER TAKE AWAY FROM US WAS OUR EDUCATION. IT HAS BEEN THE MAIN FACTOR TO SUCCEED IN THIS COUNTRY.

—*Sofia Rodriguez*

Many Cubans credit their dedication to education as a factor in enjoying a successful life in the United States.

have been integrated into the community. Still, as in any immigrant group, not all Cubans have successfully rebuilt their lives in the United States. Pockets of poverty can be found in Cuban communities.

Political Passions

Cuban Americans remain the most politically active immigrant group in the United States. Ever since the first Cuban exiles arrived in the United States, Cuban American communities have had a vibrant and sometimes controversial political life. Cuban Americans dominate the politics of South Florida. While historically most immigrant groups have voted for Democratic politicians, the majority of Cuban Americans are Republicans. Traditionally, they aligned themselves with conservative, anti-Communist lawmakers, and many Cubans continue to support Republicans' anti-Castro views. In recent years, however, the number of Cuban Democrats has grown.

Several Cuban Americans have been elected to political office. In Congress, Ileana Ros-Lehtinen and Lincoln Diaz-Balart represent districts in Florida, while Bob Menendez represents New Jersey's thirteenth Congressional District along the Hudson River.

Even Cubans who have lived in the United States for decades maintain a keen interest in politics and developments on the island. Several Cuban American political groups work to influence U.S.

Democrat Alex Penelas, former mayor of Miami-Dade County, is a rarity among Cuban American politicians, most of whom are Republicans.

policies toward Castro. Groups including the Free Cuba Foundation, the Cuban American National Foundation, and the Cuban American Alliance and Education Fund debate issues such as the U.S. trade embargo against Cuba, the future of Cuba, and U.S. immigration policy.

Many municipios still operate in Miami. Over the years, they became more concerned with political issues than with helping Cuban exiles adjust to the United States. In addition to providing citizenship information for new immigrants, the municipios focus on issues such as U.S–Cuba relations.

Many Cuban Americans—and U.S. citizens in general—favor relaxation of the U.S. government's trade and travel policies toward Cuba. A 2002 national poll found that more than two-thirds of Americans believe that they should be free to travel and sell food and medicine to Cuba. But in 2004, President George W. Bush restricted travel even further, still hoping to pressure Castro to step down. Under the new rules, Cuban Americans can go to Cuba only once every three years, and the limits on how much money they can spend there have been tightened.

Other Cuban American organizations fight for basic human rights in Cuba, such as freedom of assembly, freedom of speech, and freedom to disagree with Castro. From their base in Miami, these human rights organizations try to address the issues within Cuba. Radio Martí and Television Martí, supported by

LET ME TELL YOU, IT IS NOT EASY BEING A CUBAN-AMERICAN DEMOCRAT. IT HAS BEEN VERY, VERY DIFFICULT FOR ME TO REMAIN A DEMOCRAT BECAUSE OF THE INCREDIBLE PRESSURE I'VE GOTTEN FROM THE CUBAN-AMERICAN COMMUNITY THAT'S PREDOMINANTLY REPUBLICAN.

—Alex Penelas

the U.S. government, broadcast international news from Florida to Cuba.

Historically, the Cuban American community in Miami has taken a strong anti-Castro stance, but some of Miami's leaders are calling for more tolerance. For example, Cuban American leaders successfully lobbied to host the Latin Grammy Awards in Miami in 2003. The Florida city had previously lost out to Los Angeles. Miami officials, not wanting to provide any support to Castro's government, had tried to prevent Cuban performers from using the city's public venues.

> CUBAN MUSIC IS MY MOTHERLAND. . . . ANYONE CAN ENJOY CUBAN MUSIC—IN TROPICAL REGIONS, IN TEMPERATE CLIMATES, EVEN AS FAR AS PLANET MARS; THERE, NEITHER BATISTA NOR CASTRO HAS CONTROL.
>
> *—Rafael E. Saumell*

KEEPING TRADITIONS ALIVE

Cuban traditions are thriving in Dade County and other Cuban American communities. Cubans enjoy the foods and recipes they brought with them from the island, and Cuban Americans have a lively cultural life. Cuban music is a staple of radio stations and dance clubs. Miami, considered the Latin music capital of the world, is home to many Cuban American musicians and producers, including singer Gloria Estefan and her husband, producer Emilio Estefan.

Spanish continues to be spoken in many Cuban American households, and several Spanish-language newspapers, radio stations, and television stations serve Hispanic communities in South Florida. Older generations of Cubans in the United States are more likely to speak Spanish than are second- and third-generation Cuban Americans. These younger citizens grew up speaking English.

THE *QUINCES*

One Cuban tradition, the *quinceañera*, became even more important in the United States than in Cuba. The *quinces*, as it's called, celebrates a girl's fifteenth birthday. An important rite of passage in many Hispanic cultures, the quinces signifies that a girl has become a woman. She can go on dates and wear makeup, and she's expected to take on more responsibilities around the house.

A young girl gets ready for her quinceañera.

In Cuba the quinces was a special family occasion with plenty of good food, music, and cake. In Miami the celebration has become as much a way to show off as to welcome womanhood. Some Cubans in Miami throw elaborate quinces parties similar to weddings, featuring three-tiered cakes and girls sweeping down staircases in fancy designer dresses. Many Cuban American families, even those with modest incomes, save up for years to pay for the caterer, photographer, band, and gown.

Cuban Americans love to get together with friends and family. They may share a meal, watch a football game on TV, or celebrate birthdays, weddings, christenings, and anniversaries. For most Cuban Americans, Christmas Eve is the most important holiday of the year.

ROAST PORK

This recipe is easier to make than a traditional roast pig, but it still gives you a taste of roast pork, Cuban style. To learn how to prepare other Cuban dishes, visit www.inamericabooks.com.

4 CLOVES GARLIC, PEELED
1/4 TSP. OREGANO
1/4 TSP. SALT
1/4 TSP. BLACK PEPPER
1/2 C. SOUR ORANGE JUICE (SEE BELOW)
2 LBS. BONELESS PORK TENDERLOIN, TRIMMED

1. Mash garlic cloves, using a mortar and pestle, or a small bowl and a fork or the back of a spoon. Combine mashed garlic, oregano, salt, pepper, and sour orange juice in a large bowl to make a marinade. (You may be able to find sour orange juice in Latin American markets or specialty grocery stores. Otherwise, replace it with a mixture of 1/4 c. regular orange juice, 2 tbsp. fresh lime juice, and 2 tbsp. fresh lemon juice.) Set aside 2 tbsp. of marinade in the refrigerator.
2. Place pork in marinade and use your hands to coat meat well with marinade. Cover and refrigerate 3 to 4 hours.
3. Preheat oven to 325°F. Remove pork from marinade and place in a baking dish. Discard all but reserved 2 tbsp. of marinade.
4. Place pork in oven. Roast pork, uncovered, for 1 1/2 hours, or until a meat thermometer inserted into the center of the roast reads 155°F to 165°F. If meat looks dry during roasting, baste with a small amount of reserved marinade. Let roast cool for 10 minutes before slicing to serve.

Serves 6 to 8.

For weeks beforehand, Cuban supermarkets are stocked with Spanish cider, chestnuts, and imported Spanish nougat candy. Cuban Americans also celebrate U.S. holidays such as Thanksgiving. Instead of a turkey, however, a Cuban family is likely to have the traditional roast pig, rice and beans, and yucca.

Generational Differences

Depending on their age, year of arrival, and place of residence, Cubans in America vary in their attitudes toward Cuba and the United States. The first generation, those who left the island immediately following the revolution, identified themselves as Cubans in exile. Many remained haunted by a dream of returning to Cuba.

Their sons and daughters, most born in Cuba between 1945 and 1955, grew up in the United States with a feeling of being cut off from their roots. Many of these people came to see

My parents, who are now in their early seventies, have no choice but to be Cuban. No matter how many years they have resided away from the island . . . they are as Cuban today as they were when they got off the ferry in October 1960. My children, who were born in this country of Cuban parents and in whom I have tried to [implant] some sort of cubanía, are American through and through. . . . Like other second-generation immigrants, they maintain a connection to their parents' homeland, but it is a bond forged by my experiences rather than their own. For my children Cuba is an enduring . . . fiction.

—Gustavo Pérez Firmat

themselves as Cuban Americans, with a dual identity—a double language and cultural heritage.

Cuban Americans who were born in the United States are far more distanced from Cuba. For these "ABCs," or American-Born Cubans, the United States is home, and they have no intention of returning to Cuba, even if Communism falls and a more democratic government comes to the island. Younger Cuban Americans are more likely to take a softer stance toward Fidel Castro.

My daughter always said, "When the children come to your home, speak to them about Cuba, tell them about Cuba, because I want them to know they are part Cuban and part American, that we are proud and have a lot of things to be proud of." I am proud of my tradition, my culture.

—Irma de Leon

An Ongoing Story

Since the year 2000, the administration of President George W. Bush has continued to hold a hard line against Castro. President Bush tightened the restrictions on travel to Cuba and suspended conversations with Cuba about migration. The U.S. government has also cracked down on hijackings and illegal migration by Cubans. But Cubans continue to come to the United States through both official and unofficial channels. Many Cubans still risk their lives trying to make the journey to the United States.

The politics and identity of the first wave of Cuban immigrants revolved around anti-Communism and the hoped-for fall of Fidel Castro. In the future, Cuban Americans will be united by a broader array of issues. Castro is nearly eighty years old, and no one is sure what will happen in Cuba

FIND LINKS TO READ THE LATEST CUBAN NEWS AT WWW.INAMERICABOOKS.COM.

after his death. In the post-Castro era, Cuban Americans may no longer be defined by a sense of exile. Many Cuban Americans expect the links between the two countries to grow stronger.

As Cuban Americans continue to establish themselves in all aspects of U.S. society, they will focus more on issues closer to home and less on what's happening in Cuba. Nonetheless, younger Cuban Americans still embrace many aspects of traditional Cuban life, including the value placed on education and the family. And, like all Americans, Cuban immigrants share in the pursuit of freedom.

WE HAVE LEARNED THAT YOU DON'T HAVE TO LIVE IN CUBA TO BE CUBAN. RATHER, BEING CUBAN IS A STATE OF MIND—A VERY PARTICULAR WAY OF SEEING THE WORLD, WITH HUMOR AND *ALEGRÍA* [JOY].

—Effrain J. Ferrer and Vivan de la Incera

Famous Cuban Americans

Desi Arnaz (1917–1986) During the 1950s, Desi Arnaz became the

most famous Hispanic person in the United States when he played Ricky Ricardo on the popular *I Love Lucy* show. On TV and in real life, Arnaz was the famous comedian Lucille Ball's husband. Arnaz was born in 1917 in Santiago de Cuba, where his father was mayor. After Fulgencio Batista took power in 1933, Arnaz's family fled to Miami, Florida. Before finding fame in movies and television, Arnaz was a bandleader in Miami and New York.

Celia Cruz (ca. 1924–2003) Famous for her deep, resounding voice, singer Celia Cruz was born in

Havana around 1924. She began her singing career in Cuba in the 1940s and immigrated to the United States in 1961. She became known as the Queen of Salsa, beloved for her commanding performances.

Cameron Diaz (b. 1972) Movie star Cameron Diaz was born and raised in San Diego, California. Her father was born in Cuba and her mother is of German, English, and Native American descent. After a successful modeling career, Diaz made her film debut in the 1994 movie *Mask*. Her movie roles include *Shrek*, *Shrek 2*, *Charlie's Angels*, and *There's Something about Mary*.

Gloria Estefan (b. 1957) Popular singer Gloria Estefan was born in Havana in 1957. Her family fled to the United States in 1959.

While attending the University of Miami, Gloria met bandleader Emilio Estefan and became the band's vocalist. The two married in 1978, and in the 1980s, their band, the Miami Sound Machine, created several hit records and won numerous music awards. By the early 2000s, Estefan was an

international superstar, with more than twenty albums and five Grammy Awards.

ANDY GARCIA (b. 1956) Television and movie star Andy Garcia was born Andrés Arturo García Menéndez in Havana in 1956. He and his family left Cuba in 1961 and settled in Miami Beach, Florida. Garcia began acting while in college and moved to Hollywood in 1978. He has starred in *Hill Street Blues* on television and in many films, including *Stand and Deliver*, *The Untouchables*, *Ocean's Eleven*, and *Ocean's Twelve*.

CRISTINA GARCIA (b. 1958) Novelist Cristina Garcia was born in Havana in 1958 and moved to New York with her parents when she was two years old. After a journalism career, she turned to fiction writing in 1990. In her novels *Dreaming in Cuban* (1992), *The Aguero Sisters* (1997), and *Monkey Hunting* (2003), she explores the Cuban American experience.

ROBERTO GOIZUETA (1931–1997) The son of a sugar refinery owner, Roberto Goizueta was born in Havana in 1931. He earned a degree in chemical engineering from Yale University in 1953. The next year, he began working as a chemist for the Coca-Cola Company. He worked his way up, becoming chief executive officer in 1981, a position he held until his death in 1997.

CARLOS GUTIERREZ (b. 1953) Secretary of Commerce Carlos Gutierrez was born in Havana in 1953. After fleeing Cuba in 1960 for Miami Beach, Florida, his family eventually settled in Mexico City, Mexico. At the age of twenty, Gutierrez joined the Kellogg Company, delivering Frosted Flakes to local stores. He worked his way up at Kellogg and became chief executive officer of the company in 1999. In 2005 President George W. Bush appointed Gutierrez secretary of commerce, calling him a "great American success story."

ORLANDO HERNÁNDEZ (b. 1969) Nicknamed El Duque (the Duke), baseball player Orlando Hernández was born in Villa Clara, Cuba, in 1969. He defected (gave up his Cuban citizenship) in 1997 to play baseball in the major leagues,

following his younger half brother Liván Hernández, who is also a professional baseball player. Orlando has been a pitcher for the New York Yankees since 1998.

OSCAR HIJUELOS (b. 1951) Oscar Hijuelos was born to Cuban immigrant parents in New York City in 1951. In 1990 he won the Pulitzer Prize for his novel *The Mambo Kings Play Songs of Love.* Set in New York during the 1930s and 1940s, the book describes the adventures of the Castillo brothers, who try to strike it big with their mambo band.

JORGE MAS CANOSA (1939–1997) The son of a Cuban army officer, Jorge Mas Canosa grew up in Santiago de Cuba. He fled Cuba in 1960 and joined other Cuban exiles in 1961 to launch the unsuccessful Bay of Pigs invasion. Mas Canosa built a successful telecommunications business and became a multimillionaire. As the founder of the Cuban American National Foundation, he was the most influential leader in the Cuban American community before his death in 1997.

BOB MENENDEZ (b. 1954) A sixth-term congressperson from New Jersey, Bob Menendez is one of the Democratic Party's most prominent Latino members. Menendez was born in New York City in 1954 and raised in Union City, New Jersey. Before being elected to the U.S. House of Representatives, Menendez worked as a lawyer, was the mayor of Union City, and served in the New Jersey legislature.

MINNIE MINOSO (b. 1922) Born Saturnino Minoso in Havana in 1922, baseball legend Minnie Minoso played outfield and third base for four major league teams. Known as the Cuban Comet, Minoso broke the color barrier with the Chicago White Sox in 1951, becoming the team's first black player.

RAFAEL PALMEIRO (b. 1964) Rafael "Raffy" Palmeiro is one of baseball's heavyweight hitters, achieving his five-hundredth career

home run in 2003. Palmeiro was born in Havana in 1964 and came with his parents and two brothers to the United States in 1971. His older brother José was forced to stay behind in Cuba, and Rafael didn't see him again for more than twenty years.

NARCISO RODRIGUEZ (b. 1961) Born in New Jersey in 1961 to Cuban parents, fashion designer Narciso Rodriguez studied at Parsons School of Design in New York City. He worked for several famous designers before launching his own clothing label in 1998. Since then he has won several awards.

AGUSTÍN ROMÁN (b. 1928) Agustín Román was born in a rural area near Havana, Cuba, in 1928 and was ordained as a priest in 1959. He and 132 other Catholic priests in Cuba were expelled from the island by Fidel Castro's regime in 1961. Román ministered in Chile before coming to Miami in 1966. He took a special interest in helping Cuban exiles. He was appointed auxiliary bishop of the Archdiocese of Miami in 1979 and retired in 2003.

ILEANA ROS-LEHTINEN (b. 1952) The first Hispanic woman elected to the U.S. Congress, Ileana Ros-Lehtinen was born in Havana in 1952. When she was seven years old, her family came to the United States. After earning degrees at Florida International University, Ros-Lehtinen served as principal of a private elementary school she founded. She entered politics in 1982, serving for seven years in the Florida legislature and then winning a seat in Congress in 1989.

FÉLIX VARELA (1788–1853) Félix Varela was born in Havana in 1788 and raised in Saint Augustine, Florida. After becoming a priest, he returned to Cuba, where he was elected a deputy to the Spanish courts and legislature. He moved to New York City in 1823 and was known for his service to poor people, including thousands of Irish immigrants.

Timeline

1492 Christopher Columbus lands in Cuba.

1511 Diego Velázquez leads the Spanish conquest of Cuba. By 1514 the Spaniards have defeated the native people and established several settlements on the island.

1886 Ybor City, Florida, which became the Cigar Capital of the World, is founded by Cuban cigar makers, drawing thousands of Cuban workers.

1898 The United States joins Cuba's war with Spain after the U.S. battleship *Maine* is blown up in the Havana harbor. The United States defeats Spain in less than four months and takes control of Cuba.

1953 On July 26, a young lawyer named Fidel Castro leads an unsuccessful attack on the Moncada army barracks in Santiago de Cuba, hoping to overthrow Batista's government.

1959 Castro takes power in Cuba. The first major wave of Cuban migration to the United States begins.

1960 The United States enacts a trade embargo against Cuba.

1961 Castro declares that Cuba is a Communist nation. Cuban exiles, backed by the U.S. government, invade Cuba at the Bay of Pigs but are defeated by Castro's army.

1962 The U.S. government sets up the Cuban Refugee Program in Miami to help Cuban exiles adjust to their new surroundings. In October U.S. president John F. Kennedy learns that Soviet missiles are being installed in Cuba. The missile crisis ends when the arms are removed and the United States agrees not to invade Cuba.

1965–1973	Freedom Flights between Cuba and Florida bring more than 300,000 Cubans to the United States.
1980	Castro announces that boats from the United States can pick up Cuban refugees at the port of Mariel, Cuba. During the Mariel Boatlift, more than 125,000 Cubans migrate to the United States.
1989	Ileana Ros-Lehtinen becomes the first Cuban American elected to the U.S. Congress.
1994	Castro declares that the Cuban government will no longer try to prevent Cubans from leaving the island by boat. Thousands of balseros, or rafters, leave on handmade crafts. Cuba and the United States reach an agreement in which the United States will admit twenty thousand Cuban immigrants a year. In return, Cuba pledges to do more to prevent illegal departures.
1996	Cuba shoots down two U.S. civilian aircraft piloted by Cuban exiles. The U.S. Congress passes the Helms-Burton Act, which tightens the trade embargo even more.
1999	The Cuban American community rallies to keep Elián González in the United States after the six-year-old Cuban boy is rescued off the Florida coast.
2000	Elián is returned to his father in Cuba, leading to outrage among Cuban Americans.
2004	President George W. Bush tightens restrictions on travel to Cuba.

Glossary

ASYLUM: protection given by one country to a political refugee from another country

COMMUNISM: a political and economic system in which resources and property are owned and shared equally by the whole community. Communism is based on the theories of Karl Marx, Friedrich Engels, and Vladimir Lenin, who promoted the ideal of a classless society.

CUBANIDAD: Cuban identity; a sense of "Cubanness," or what it means to be Cuban

DICTATOR: a leader who holds complete control and often rules by not allowing any opposition or disagreement

EMIGRATE: to leave one's homeland to live in another country. A person who emigrates is called an emigrant.

EXILE: a forced absence from one's country or home; being banished or sent out of one's country. The word also refers to a person who is in exile.

IMMIGRATE: to come to live in a country other than one's homeland. A person who immigrates is called an immigrant.

RATIONING: providing food and consumer goods in fixed quantities at certain specified times

REFUGEE: a person who flees to a foreign country to escape danger or political punishment or repression

REPRESSION: prevention or forceful curbing of freedoms, such as free expression

SALSA: a high-energy Latin American dance music with elements of Afro-Cuban rhythms, jazz, and other musical forms

SOCIALISM: an economic system in which the government controls most industries

TRADE EMBARGO: a government order forbidding the export and import of goods to and from a country or territory

Things to See and Do

Calle Ocho Festival, Miami, Florida
http://www.carnaval-miami.org/start.htm
Every year in March, the Little Havana neighborhood in Miami holds a massive street festival. (Calle Ocho, or Southwest Eighth Street, is the heart of Little Havana.) Similar in spirit to the Carnival festivals held in Havana, Santiago, and other Latin American cities, el Festival de la Ocho, as it's commonly called, celebrates Hispanic culture in the United States. Entire streets are blocked off to make room for music, dance, arts, food, and other fun.

Cuban-American Music Festival, Los Angeles, California
This celebration of Cuban culture takes place in Echo Park in Los Angeles on a Sunday in May. The festival showcases Cuban art, culture, music, and food. Musical acts perform salsa, Latin jazz, and other Cuban and Afro-Cuban styles.

Freedom Tower, Miami, Florida
Often referred to as Miami's Ellis Island, this restored tower on Biscayne Boulevard was the first stop for nearly 400,000 Cuban refugees who arrived in South Florida from the early 1960s through the 1970s. A symbol of freedom, the tower is a museum for historical exhibits and serves as a site for rallies, protests, marches, and prayer vigils by Cuban Americans.

Little Havana, Miami, Florida
Located along and around Southwest Eighth Street, Little Havana is a twenty-five-block neighborhood that has served as the center of the Cuban community in the United States since the early 1960s. The streets of Little Havana are lined with Cuban cafés, clubs, shops, car dealerships, and other businesses. The Calle Ocho Walk of Fame gives stars to Latin celebrities.

Ybor City, Tampa, Florida Ybor City, the former Cigar Capital of the World, is a National Historic Landmark District. Brick streets are lined with cast-iron street lamps, and buildings have wrought-iron balconies and decorative bricks. A few of the cottages that once housed cigar workers are part of the Ybor City State Museum, while a renovated cigar factory is home to Ybor Square, a mall filled with restaurants and shops.

Source Notes

7 Jaime Suchlicki, *Cuba: From Columbus to Castro and Beyond*, 4th ed. (Washington, DC: Brasseys, 1997), 3.

10 Gustavo Pérez Firmat, *Life on the Hyphen: The Cuban-American Way* (Austin: University of Texas Press, 1994), 10.

13 Alex Antón and Roger E. Hernández, *Cubans in America: A Vibrant History of a People in Exile* (New York: Kensington Books, 2002), 63.

16 Dorothy Hoobler and Thomas Hoobler, *The Cuban American Family Album* (New York: Oxford University Press, 1996), 16.

22 Ibid., 18.

26 Ibid., 23.

29 Miguel Gonzalez-Pando, *The Cuban Americans* (Westport, CT: The Greenwood Press, 1998), 40.

30 Hoobler and Hoobler, 31.

32 Ibid., 51.

33 Gonzalez-Pando, 41.

36 James S. Olson and Judith E. Olson, *Cuban Americans: From Trauma to Triumph* (New York: Twayne Publishers, 1995), 65.

38 Gonzalez-Pando, 47.

38 Ibid., 37.

38. Andrea O'Reilly Herrera, ed., *ReMembering Cuba: Legacy of a Diaspora* (Austin: University of Texas Press, 2001), 68.

39 Gonzalez-Pando, 155.

40 Herrera, 38.

45 Ibid., 33.

49 Hoobler and Hoobler, 37.

54 "Versailles Restaurant," *Three Guys from Miami: A Cuban Insider's Guide to Miami*, August 4, 2004, http://icuban.com/3guys/versailles.html (January 31, 2005).

55 Gonzalez-Pando, x.

57 Hoobler and Hoobler, 86.

59 Adam C. Smith, "Alex Penelas Confronts a Tough Critic: His Own Party," *St. Petersburg Times*, August 31, 2003, http://www.sptimes.com/2003/08/31/Perspective/Alex_Penelas_confronts.html (July 30, 2004).

60 Herrera, 12.

63 Pérez Firmat, 5.

64 Hoobler and Hoobler, 116.

65 Herrera, 33.

Selected Bibliography

Antón, Alex, and Roger E. Hernández. *Cubans in America: A Vibrant History of a People in Exile.* New York: Kensington Books, 2002. This lively book traces the history of Cubans in America.

Gonzalez-Pando, Miguel. *The Cuban Americans.* Westport, CT: The Greenwood Press, 1998. This book provides historical background on Cuban migration and discusses the development of a Cuban exile community in the United States.

Herrera, Andrea O'Reilly, ed. *ReMembering Cuba: Legacy of a Diaspora.* Austin: University of Texas Press, 2001. This collection of essays and interviews explores what it means to be a Cuban American.

Morey, Janet Nomura, and Wendy Dunn. *Famous Hispanic Americans.* New York: Cobblehill Books, 1996. This collection of biographies of famous Hispanic Americans includes Gloria Estefan, Andy Garcia, Roberto Goizueta, Lourdes Lopez, and Ileana Ros-Lehtinen.

Olson, James S., and Judith E. Olson. *Cuban Americans: From Trauma to Triumph.* New York: Twayne Publishers, 1995. This thorough history of Cuban immigration includes an overview of Cuban history and a discussion of Cuban migration from the late 1800s to 1995.

Pérez Firmat, Gustavo. *Life on the Hyphen: The Cuban-American Way.* Austin: University of Texas Press, 1994. Written by a member of the "1.5 generation"—Cubans who came to the United States as children or adolescents—this book discusses the ways Cubans have affected American culture and vice versa.

Robson, Barbara. "Cubans: Their History and Culture." *Cultural Orientation Project.* 1996. http://www.culturalorientation.net/cubans/ (July 26, 2004). Events that have prompted Cuban immigration to the United States are discussed in this thorough guide to Cuban American history and culture.

U.S. Census Bureau. "Profiles of General Demographic Characteristics." Census 2000 Gateway. May 2001. http://www2.census.gov/census_2000/datasets/demographic_profile/0_National_Summary/2khus.pdf (August 31, 2004). This document provides details on American ethnicity and population.

Further Reading & Websites

Nonfiction

Behnke, Alison, and Victor Manuel Valens. *Cooking the Cuban Way.* Minneapolis: Lerner Publications Company, 2004. This cultural cookbook presents recipes for authentic and traditional Cuban dishes, including holiday recipes.

Butts, Ellen, and Joyce Schwartz. *Fidel Castro.* Minneapolis: Lerner Publications Company, 2005. This biography tells the life story of the man who has ruled Cuba as a Communist nation since 1959.

Campbell, Kumari. *Cuba in Pictures.* Minneapolis: Lerner Publications Company, 2004. Information about the geography, history, people, economics, and culture of Cuba is provided in this thorough overview.

Eire, Carlos. *Waiting for Snow in Havana: Confessions of a Cuban Boy.* New York: Free Press, 2002. In a moving, wry memoir, the author discusses his childhood in Havana before being flown out of Cuba at the age of eleven.

Hoobler, Dorothy, and Thomas Hoobler. *The Cuban American Family Album.* New York: Oxford University Press, 1996. The history of Cuban immigration to the United States is told through stories and quotes from Cubans who made the journey.

Pérez Firmat, Gustavo. *Next Year in Cuba: A Cubano's Coming-of-Age in America.* New York: Anchor Books, 1996. This touching, personal account describes a young Cuban American's struggle to find his identity as he straddles two cultures.

Fiction

Garcia, Cristina. *Dreaming in Cuban.* New York: Knopf, 1992. The stories of three generations of Cuban women are told in this novel about the Cuban American experience.

García, Cristina, ed. *¡Cubanísimo!* New York: Vintage Books, 2003. This collection of stories, poems, essays, and novel excerpts captures the spirit and diversity of Cuban culture.

Menéndez, Ana. *In Cuba I Was a German Shepherd.* New York: Grove

Press, 2001. These linked short stories focus on Cuban immigrants as they make new lives in Miami.

Osa, Nancy. *Cuba 15*. New York: Delacorte Books for Young Readers, 2003. As Violet Paz, a tenth-grader in suburban Chicago, gets ready to have her quinceañera, she becomes eager to learn more about her Cuban roots.

Veciana-Suarez, Ana. *Flight to Freedom*. New York: Orchard Books, 2002. Told in diary form, this novel tells the story of thirteen-year-old Yara Garcia and her family as they flee Cuba for a new life in Miami.

Websites

Cuban Heritage Collection
http://www.library.miami.edu/umcuban/cuban.html
This site describes a collection of rare books, journals, newspapers, postcards, photographs, maps, posters, and other materials from Cuba's early colonial period through the present.

HispanicOnline.com
http://www.hispaniconline.com
This portal site provides access to a wide variety of information and resources for Hispanic Americans, including sections on politics, arts and entertainment, business, careers, and sports.

HistoryOfCuba.Com
http://historyofcuba.com/cuba.htm
Cuban history comes to life on this site, which includes an interactive timetable of more than five hundred years of Cuba's past.

iCuban.com: The Internet Cuban
http://www.icuban.com
One of the most popular Cuban sites, iCuban.com provides information about Cuban culture from the Three Guys from Miami, brothers-in-law who share their tips on food, recipes, and travel.

inamericabooks.com
http://www.inamericabooks.com
Visit inamericabooks.com, the online home of the In America series, to get linked to all sorts of useful information. You'll find historical and cultural websites related to individual groups, as well as general information on genealogy, creating your own family tree, and the history of immigration in America.

INDEX

ACKNOWLEDGMENTS: THE PHOTOGRAPHS IN THIS BOOK ARE REPRODUCED WITH THE PERMISSION OF: © Digital Vision Royalty Free, pp. 1, 3, 24; © Samuel Lund, pp. 6, 19, 39, 54; © Dave G. Houser/CORBIS, p. 7; © James Ford Bell Library, University of Minnesota, p. 9; © CORBIS, p. 11; © Library of Congress, pp. 12 (LC-USZ62-101602), 14 (LC-USZ62-80); © John R. Kreul/ Independent Picture Service, p. 15; © Bettmann/CORBIS, p. 17; © Getty Images, pp. 22, 48; © Alan Schein Photography/ CORBIS, p. 25; © Kurt Severin/Three Lions/Getty Images, p. 31; © Nik Wheeler/CORBIS, pp. 34, 46; © Tony Arruza/CORBIS, p. 35; © AP|Wide World Photos, p. 37; © Tim Chapman/Miami Herald/Getty Images, p. 44; © Reuters/CORBIS, pp. 51, 69 (right); © Robert Holmes/CORBIS, p. 53; © Nathan Benn/ CORBIS, p. 57; © Miami Herald/Getty Images, p. 58; © Joe Raedle/Getty Images, p. 61; © ZUMA Press, p. 66 (top); © JDEVE/ Queen/ZUMA Press, p. 66 (bottom-left); © Paul Fenton-KPA/ KEYSTONE Pictures/ZUMA Press, p. 66 (bottom-right); © Lisa O'Connor/ZUMA Press, p. 67 (left); © Anthony J. Causi/Icon SMI/ZUMA Press, p. 68 (left); © Russ Reed/The Sporting News/ ZUMA Press, p. 68 (right); © Nancy Kaszerman/ZUMA Press, p. 69 (left); Map by Bill Hauser, p. 21.

Cover photo: AP|Wide World Photos, (top); © Samuel Lund, (bottom-right); © Digital Vision Royalty Free, (title).
Back cover photo: © Digital Vision.